MEXICO
MYSTERY

By W. A. Sorrells

Illustrations by
Tom Bancroft and Rob Corley

KARITO Kids™

Published by KidsGive, LLC
5757 W. Century Blvd., Suite 800, Box 8
Los Angeles, California 90045

Karito Kids™ and KidsGive™ are trademarks of KidsGive, LLC.

Cover art by Funny Pages Productions, LLC (Tom Bancroft,
Rob Corley, and Jon Conkling)
Interior illustrations by Funny Pages Productions, LLC
(Tom Bancroft and Rob Corley)
Journal created by Wendy Tigerman
Interior design by Andrea Reider, Reider Publishing Services

ISBN 978-0-9792912-4-1

Printed in China. First printing, 2007.

Visit Karito Kids at karitokids.com.

The first books in the series of Karito Kids™ Adventures are dedicated to Steve and Jeff for their constant support and belief in KidsGive; Hannah and Will for their enthusiasm for KidsGive's goal of helping children around the world; Dave for his commitment and friendship; Andrea for her awesome work and dedication; Janet for her humor and belief in us; and last, but most certainly not least, Julie for her spirit and chutzpah. We couldn't have done it without you. Thank you for helping us imagine, create, and become.

—Love, Laura and Lisa

Your Code Number is 895572001094.

MORE THAN JUST A BOOK
Find Out All The Ways To Enjoy This Mystery Adventure

Each Karito Kids™ Adventure is much more than simply a book. By reading this book and visiting karitokids.com, you can explore countries, solve mysteries, and best of all help kids in need in other parts of the world. Get to know all the Karito Kids and become a part of an exciting new community of kids who care!

1. **Activate Your Charitable Donation**. If you purchased this book with a Karito Kids Doll, you may have already activated your donation. If you purchased this book by itself, go to karitokids.com and follow the online instructions to activate your donation. Three percent of the price of this book will be donated by KidsGive on your behalf to the children's charity Plan. The best part is that you will get to choose the cause to which you want your donation to go. You decide how you want to make a difference!

2. **Go to karitokids.com.** Check out our Karito Kids Book Blog where you can learn more about your favorite characters, where they live, and other fun stuff. You can even share what you think about each adventure, the actions they took, and the choices they made. You can find out what other kids think, too!

3. **Look For Culture Crossings**. While you're reading this story, keep your eyes open for places in the book where another country or culture is mentioned. Located within the story, illustrations, or journal, these places are called "Culture Crossings." When you locate a place in the book where another country (other than the country the story is about) is mentioned, go to karitokids. com and visit the "Culture Crossings" area and follow the online instructions. As with all Karito Kids games, you will also earn virtual *World Change* that can be accumulated and then donated by KidsGive on your behalf (as real money) to Plan. You might also find a few surprises!

4. **Solve Hidden Quests**. Each Karito Kid has so many adventures to share. Log onto karitokids.com and visit the "Hidden Quest" area to join her on additional quests. Just as with "Culture Crossings," you can earn virtual *World Change* that can be accumulated and donated by KidsGive on your behalf (as real money) to Plan.

Join up with other kids who are *Playing for World Change!*_{sm}

WHAT IS KARITO KIDS™ ALL ABOUT?

We launched Karito Kids™ to help connect children around the world in a number of ways.

◉ The word "Karito" means charity and love of one's neighbor in the constructed language Esperanto. We hope that children around the world strengthen their connection with each other, creating a global village of peace and understanding.

◉ Each Karito Kids Doll helps children recognize and appreciate the beauty of the world's many different ethnicities.

◉ The book that accompanies each Karito Kid tells a fun story involving that girl. It brings to life another country and its culture and connects readers to the notion that children from across the world have many fundamental similarities.

◉ The unique online activation process will allow children to directly participate in giving. They can determine the cause to which they wish to direct a percentage of the purchase price of the product. They can receive updates on the project they choose and find out how they helped children somewhere else in the world.

◉ Combining traditional play with innovative interactive games provides your child a play date with kids all over the world. They will have the opportunity to write to children sponsored by KidsGive and learn how children live in other parts of the world.

◉ Our selected charity, Plan, is a non-profit organization that is bringing hope and help to more than 10 million children and their families in poor communities worldwide. KidsGive contributes 3% of the retail price to one charity to maximize the impact of change.

uno

Buenas dias. I am very pleased to meet you. My name is Agapita Maria Reña Corta, but you may call me Pita. I live in Mexico City. I am eleven years old, have long brown hair and brown eyes, and stand 1.46 meters tall. That's the same as four feet three inches.

My favorite things are horses, books, horses, friends and horses. Did I mention I like horses?

I am the luckiest girl in the world. Mexico is a poor country, but I have everything I could possibly want. My father is Gabriel Reña Garcia. Perhaps you have heard of him. He is a member of the Mexican Senate. My mother is Elizabet Corta de Reña. She used to be a model, but now she is a famous hostess in Mexico City. They are the best parents in the world.

Except they never let me do anything that I want to do.

But other than that, my life is perfect.

My horse, Estrella, and I are members of the Asociacion Federal de Equitacion (Federal Equestrian Society), the most famous horse club in Mexico. Estrella means "star" in Spanish.

One summer day, I was riding with my friends Rosa and Susan. Rosa's father owns a very large company that makes automobile parts, and Susan's father is the American ambassador to Mexico. Susan is very naughty. As you will see.

Rosa's bodyguard, Manuel, was riding in front of us, and my bodyguard, Omar, was riding behind us as we rode through the woods. In the United States, the President's child might have a bodyguard, but in Mexico many important people with money use bodyguards. "Slowly, girls!" Omar called. "You're riding too fast."

Omar says this about ninety times when we go riding. It's very boring to ride slowly, but he knows that if I fall off the horse, he will probably get fired.

Susan knows that Omar speaks only Spanish, so she leaned toward me and said in English. "This is so boooooooring!"

I must admit, I had to agree. Omar rides way too slow. Omar is a nice guy, but he's no fun at all.

"When we reach that fork in the trail," Susan

said, "let's go to the right."

Rosa was not a very good rider, so she shook her head. "No way!"

"Scaredy cat!" Susan said.

Rosa shook her head. "It's not like that," she explained. "We just have to be careful. We're not supposed to leave the bodyguards."

We were approaching the fork in the trail. We always took the left path when we went riding.

"I'm going to the right," Susan said. "I don't care."

"But we'll get in trouble!" Rosa whined.

Susan made chicken noises. "Bwwwwwaack-bwack-bwack-bwwwaaaaack!"

Every time we came to the fork in the trail, I wondered where the right path led. It was narrow and weedy and obviously not used very much.

It disappeared very quickly into the trees. But it never really occurred to me to ride that way. Not until Susan said something about it.

"We can't!" Rosa said.

"Come on, Pita," Susan said. "Don't be a chicken."

"Anyway, I told you we're leaving for Cuernavaca today," I said. "I can't be late."

"Chicken! Chicken! Bwaaaaack-bwack-bwack!" Susan clucked. "You'll be at your grandfather's house all summer. We won't see you again until school starts in August. A little extra time in Mexico City can't hurt."

I sat up very straight and kept looking ahead. This is how I was taught to ride. Very correctly. I ride English style. Susan, on the other hand, is very slouchy and rides Western style. She's from Texas and wears a cowboy hat and these cool snakeskin cowboy boots with pictures of snakes tooled into the leather. My mother would never let me wear boots like that. When I ride, I wear jodhpurs, my riding helmet, a crisp white shirt, and high black riding boots. Our maid shines the boots so that I can almost see myself in them.

Manuel reached the fork and kept going to the left. Then Rosa went left. Susan was headed in that direction, then suddenly she pulled off her cowboy hat and whacked it on her horse's neck.

"Yahhhh!" she howled. Her horse leapt to the right.

I don't know what I was thinking. I meant to keep going in the right direction. But the next thing I knew, I had dug my heels into Estrella's flanks and tugged the reins. I was flying down the wrong path behind Susan. Estrella galloped at top speed, and I bumped up and down. Branches whacked me in the face, and my heart was beating so hard it felt like I was going to burst right out of the saddle.

What am I doing? I thought. I was so used to doing the right thing, I hardly knew what it was like to break the rules.

"Girls! Come back here!" Our bodyguards were shouting frantically at us. But neither Manuel nor Omar was as good a rider as Susan and I. So, within a minute, we'd left them behind. There were several more forks in the trail, and suddenly we were getting very deep into the woods.

I couldn't even think. I just hung on and followed Susan's blonde ponytail.

"See?" Susan called over the pounding of the

horses' hooves. "Isn't this better? Back in America, people like us can do anything we want. We can go to the store, go to the park, do anything. Here, I feel like I'm in prison. Don't you wish it was like this all the time?"

Looking at the path ahead of us, I wasn't sure. The trail got narrower and darker, and I got more and more scared.

Finally Susan slowed down, looked back, and flashed me a grin. The horses cantered down the path. We were going up and down hills now, and I couldn't even hear Manuel or Omar behind us.

Suddenly Susan's horse stopped, then neighed in terror. Estrella and I barely avoided slamming into them.

"Uh-oh," Susan said softly. Her face had gone white.

For a moment I wondered why Susan had stopped so quickly. Then I saw it. We were on the edge of a cliff. Stretched out below us was the vast, polluted, hazy vista of Mexico City, one of the largest cities in the world. If Susan's horse hadn't pulled up short, we both probably would have plunged thirty meters down the hill.

In the canyon below was a town. I had never seen anything like it. The houses made

of cardboard boxes, scrap lumber, and pieces of rusting corrugated iron were crammed together.

Stinking smoke drifted up to us. A woman wearing the bright clothes of an Indian from southern Mexico was burning garbage in a black oil drum. Shoeless kids looked up and pointed at us, then yelled something that I couldn't hear.

"What is this?" I whispered.

Susan shook her head. "I don't know."

I had never seen anything like it. In many neighborhoods in Mexico City, people with money live right next to people with very little money. Mansions tower over smaller houses on the same block. But there were no mansions here.

"Susan. Agapita." Manuel and Omar's shouts echoed in the distance. "Let's get out of here," Susan said.

I pulled on Estrella's reins and turned around.

dos

When we got back to the house, everyone was already packed up and ready to go. We live in a very large house surrounded by a wall topped with barbed wire in the Lomas de Chapultepec section of Mexico City. A long line of vehicles sat in front of the house. Our bodyguards rode in two black Jeeps. The black Chevy Suburban was for our maid, Evita, and her husband, Carlos. Estrella would ride in a horse trailer behind a large pick-up truck. My father's assistants rode in a black Cadillac. The Mercedes limousine was for me, Papa, Mama, and of course Mama's little dog, Maximilian, to ride in.

Omar didn't tell Mama and Papa what had happened earlier. I could tell Papa was very angry because we were late. He didn't say anything to me, though. He just glared at his watch, and kept talking on his cell phone.

"How was your ride?" Mama said as we settled into the Mercedes. As always, Mama was dressed perfectly. Her hair was perfect. Her makeup was perfect. A single strand of pearls hung around her neck. Maximilian sat on her lap. He was a Pomeranian, with that kind of hair that hangs down over his face. His hair was perfect, too.

"Fine," I said. But I still felt queasy. Seeing that cardboard town had bothered me.

"Are you looking forward to seeing Abuelo?" Mama said to me.

I laughed. "Of course!" I said. I was crazy about my grandfather, or Tata, which is what I call him. Mama calls my grandfather Abuelo which is much more formal than my name for him. My grandmother had died when I was a baby, so I had never known her.

The truth was, I was looking forward to getting out of Mexico City, period. Sometimes I was jealous of my older brothers and sisters. (I have five of them!) They were already adults, with jobs and children. There were times when I wished I was old enough to go off on my own, too. Then again my older brothers and sisters didn't get to spend summers with Tata.

My life with my parents still was always about what I *couldn't* do. I couldn't go anywhere without a bodyguard, because it was too dangerous. But the bodyguards weren't the only problem. Mother had a million rules about what was right and what was wrong to do in Mexico City. She's got strong ideas about how things are supposed to be. A thing was either *correcto* or it was not. If it was not *correcto,* then it was either "dangerous" or "common."

As we got into the limousine, Maximilian jumped out of my mother's arms and ran after a squirrel. Omar and my mother's bodyguard chased after him. Mama and I laughed at the sight of two grown men chasing a dog chasing a squirrel.

When the squirrel raced up a tree, Max waited at the bottom, panting. Omar bent down and grabbed him in his big arms, then handed him over to Mama.

"Bad Max!" Mama shook her finger at the little Pomeranian. He looked at her with his innocent brown eyes, but she didn't fall for his act. "Bad boy!"

The caravan pulled out of the driveway and drove through Mexico City. We rode in the middle with the bodyguards' Jeeps right in front and behind us. Once we got going, we didn't stop for traffic lights or anything.

I daydreamed about what it would be like

once we got to Cuernavaca, the city near my
grandfather's home. Everything would relax a
little. I could go outside and walk around without
Omar trailing after me. I could occasionally wear
clothes that my mother didn't pick out.

Once I even went to a movie with my
grandfather. Afterward we sat in a restaurant near
the big square in the center of town. Tata and I
laughed and talked, and I got a Jarritos Mandarina
drink, which Mama never lets me drink.

I stopped daydreaming when a big truck pulled
out in front of us. The entire caravan stopped. For
the first time since I'd arrived back home, Papa
stopped talking on his phone. Mama got very quiet.
My father's bodyguard, who sat in the front seat,
started talking urgently on his radio.

"Is everything okay?" I said.

"It's fine, *mija,*" Mama said. But I could tell from the stiff look on her face that she was worried.

Soon the truck moved, and we started going again.

Within minutes, we got onto the main highway leading down to Cuernavaca. Mama and I talked all the way down to the city. She talked about the big party she was planning next month. She was on pins and needles about whether the president of Mexico would come or not. She talked about whether she should go to New York or Milan to buy her dress for the party. She talked about how boring it was in Cuernavaca.

My father talked on his phone the whole time. He had a personal organizer with a list of calls he needed to make. Each time he hung up the phone, he checked them off, one by one.

"*Perfecto!*" Papa said as we pulled through the gate that led to my grandfather's *hacienda,* a ranch outside Cuernavaca. "I got all my calls made. Now I can relax!" He smiled.

But Papa didn't look very relaxed. He looked at his watch. Then he looked out the window and sighed. Then he looked at his watch again.

As we pulled up in front of the house, an old Spanish colonial stucco house, my grandfather came out of the front door. He was waving right at me, a broad grin splitting his face, which was creased and lined from years of work outside. He runs a very large construction firm and he spends a lot of time out in the sun. I jumped out of the car and ran to see him.

"Pita!" he shouted, giving me a huge hug. My grandfather is a short man with black hair—even though he's almost seventy years old. Tata shook hands very formally with my father and called him "Senator." Then he kissed my mother on both cheeks. "Come in! Come in!" Tata said. Tata ordered some drinks from one of his servants, then took us out back to see the new swimming pool. Just then I heard Omar shouting something from the front of the house. It sounded like he was saying, "Estrella!"

"Let's go inside," Papa said nervously.

But I immediately started running around the side of the house to see what was going on.

"Pita!" Mama called. "Get back here."

I didn't mean to disobey Mama and Papa, but I was worried about my horse. When I got around to the front of the house, I saw our bodyguards clustered around the horse trailer. One of them was talking urgently on his walkie-talkie.

"What happened?" I called.

Omar turned and looked nervously at me.

I ran around the trailer. The rear gate was open.

The trailer was empty.

"Estrella's gone!" Omar said.

CHAPTER THREE

tres

N obody knows anything!" my father fumed, pacing up and down in Tata's living room. "How is that possible?"

"Senator, I don't see how she could have gotten out here at the hacienda," Omar was saying. "I think she must have gotten out during the drive."

"How?" my father said. "Explain this to me!"

"I don't know, sir. The trailer was the last vehicle in the caravan. Maybe when that truck pulled out in front of us, somebody took her."

"But wouldn't the driver of the truck have seen that?" Mama said.

"Please," Papa said. "I'm handling this."

Mama pursed her lips and looked away.

"I can't say, sir," Omar said. "All I know is that we were busy unloading the cars. When the groom came to unload Estrella, the gate was open and she was gone."

Papa sighed loudly. "And no one saw her?"

Omar shook his head. "No, sir."

My father frowned. "That horse cost a great deal of money," he said. "I suppose the police will have to be notified. Make the call, Omar."

I ran to my room and spent the rest of the afternoon lying face down on my bed, crying. Mama tried to console me. Tata came in and made funny faces. But it didn't do any good at all.

Finally Papa tried. "If we can't find her, I'll buy you a new horse," he said.

I knew my father was trying to be kind, but he didn't understand. "I don't want a new horse!" I shouted. "I want Estrella!" I expected my father to get angry. I had never dared raise my voice to him before.

Instead he stayed calm. "I'll buy you a better one," Papa said in a gentle voice.

"There isn't a better horse," I cried. "Estrella's the best horse in the world!"

The police arrived a little before supper.

A thin, distinguished looking man with graying sideburns introduced himself as the assistant police chief for the state police.

"Buenos noches, Senator," he said. "I'm very sorry to hear about your daughter's horse." He motioned toward a short man with dark skin,

Indian features, and watchful black eyes. There was a large scar across his neck. "This is my best investigator, Sergeant Borges."

"Senator," Sergeant Borges said. Something about him made me nervous.

"I trust you will allow me to question your staff." He had an odd whispery voice. "Of course," Papa said.

"Before I begin, is there anyone whose loyalty you would question?"

"They would not be here if I did!" Papa said sharply.

"I only mention it," Sergeant Borges said, "because in many of these kinds of cases, it's an inside job."

"That may be true," Papa said. "But right now I suspect that a simple mistake was made. Someone left the trailer gate unlatched and the horse simply wandered out."

"Sir," Omar said, "I secured the door myself. I'm quite sure—"

Papa gave Omar a look, and Omar clamped his mouth shut.

"We'll alert the local officers in this zone to be on the lookout," the sergeant said.

"It's a brown thoroughbred mare with a white

face," my father said. "Very distinctive."

Sergeant Borges cleared his throat. "I suspect, Senator, that a modest reward might be productive in arousing interest."

"I'll make sure that anyone who finds her is well taken care of," Papa said sourly.

"Excellent," the sergeant said. "If you'll permit me, I will begin questioning the staff."

Papa nodded.

After the policemen left, Tata clapped his hands "Let's eat," he said. "It never pays to worry on an empty stomach."

We went into the dining room to eat supper. Everyone was quiet at dinner. "Did you see that I had the staff prepare your favorite food, Pita?" Tata asked with a smile.

I looked down at my plate. I hadn't even taken a bite of my *mole poblano de guajolote*. Mole is a kind of sauce that's made of chile peppers, nuts, spices, and chocolate. The mole was poured over turkey. I felt bad that I hadn't even realized he'd tried to make my meal special. I took a tiny bite, but I was too upset to eat.

"For dessert," Tata added, "we'll have *crepas de cajeta*." Usually that news would have perked me right up. Nothing made my mouth water like those thin pancakes covered in caramel. But tonight even Tata and his treats couldn't make me less gloomy.

The police sergeant entered the dining room. "Excuse me, Senator," he said in his odd whispery voice. "Perhaps you should have a look at this." He handed my father a piece of paper. "This was in the mailbox."

My father read the paper, then said, "You should fingerprint this."

The sergeant stroked his jaw. "In these kinds of things, Senator, I think it would be unnecessary. If you will permit me, it might be best if I simply handled matters on your behalf."

My father stood up in his place at the table. "Would you excuse us?"

"Is it a clue?" I said hopefully. "Does someone know where she is?"

"We'll discuss it later!" he said. "This is a matter for grown-ups to discuss." He walked out of the room with Sergeant Borges following on his heels.

I started to follow them.

"Pita," Mama said. "Finish your dinner. Your plate is full."

Slowly, I sat back and pushed my meal around

with my fork. I was desperate to know what was in that note.

After about fifteen minutes, I heard the front door shut.

"What happened, Papa?" I called, running out of the dining room.

By the time I found Papa, he was already on the telephone. He put his hand over the mouthpiece and said, "It's past your bedtime." Then he called to our maid. "Evita, put her to bed now. She's had an exhausting day."

"Yes, sir," Evita said.

"What happened to Estrella?" I wailed.

"She'll be fine," my father said. Then he started talking into the phone again.

That night I snuck out of bed and into the dining room. The house seemed unnaturally quiet.

I found the piece of paper still sitting on the dining room table.

It was a note written in very messy handwriting. It looked like a child had written it. It read:

Dear Senator Reña,

We have something you want! It is a butiful horse. It is surely worth one million pesos!

Drop off the money at dimmind rock on tomorrow at 10:00 sharp. Or else!!

SIGNED,

THE DARK MOON GANG

Estrella had been kidnapped!

cuatro

The next morning at breakfast my grandfather said, "Pita, maybe you and I should go down to the stables and see where Estrella is going to stay when she gets back."

"How do you know—"

Tata put one finger over his lips. "Don't worry. You'll get Estrella back. I feel sure of it."

We walked into the sunshine toward the stables. Cuernavaca is known as the "City of Eternal Spring" because the weather is so nice. It's nestled into a valley next to a line of old volcanoes. The ranch was to the south and west of the city, way out in the country. You could see the mountains from the back of Tata's ranch. The land he lives on is dry and brown, but the mountains are green and lush, like a pile of emeralds on the horizon.

"I hired a new manager for the stables," Tata said. "And he's got a daughter your age. She's quite a little horsewoman, too."

We walked into the barn and found a tall man with bright red hair currying an Appaloosa. "Buenos dias, Señor Reña!" the man said. "This must be your granddaughter!"

"Pita, meet Diego Flynn," Tata said.

"It's a pleasure to meet you," the stable manager said to me.

I stared at him, unable to speak.

"Go ahead," Tata coaxed. "Say hello."

"It's just—" I started. "I expected you to have an accent. I thought you were American."

The man laughed. "You don't see red hair like this every day, do you?" he said. "My grandparents moved here from Ireland a long time ago. I've lived here all my life. I'm as Mexican as you are."

As he spoke, a horse ambled into the stable. "I've exercised Magnifico," the girl on its back said. "Want me to exercise any of the other horses?"

"This is my daughter, Asuncion," the stable manager said. "Asuncion, meet Pita."

Flying out from beneath a cowboy hat, the girl's hair was even redder than her father's, and she had freckled skin. "Hola," she said to me.

"I've got an idea," Tata said. "Asuncion helps

her father exercise my horses to keep them in shape. Why don't you help her?"

I half-nodded. I could tell Tata was just trying to keep my mind off Estrella, and I was certain nothing would work.

"Okay, then!" Diego Flynn said. "Excellent! Can you ride Western style, Pita?"

"Uh, sure," I said. I hardly ever rode Western. It's pretty different from riding English style. Different saddle, different everything. But Asuncion looked like a pro as she dismounted and started uncinching the saddle, so I didn't want to admit that I didn't really know what I was doing.

"Let her take Montoya," Tata said, pointing to a small Appaloosa.

"Saddle her up," Diego said.

When I rode, one of the grooms at the club normally saddled and bridled the horse for me. And Western saddles are different from English saddles anyway. "Uh..." I said.

"I'll do it," Asuncion said. She didn't say anything else, but as she saddled both our horses with quick, efficient moves, I could tell she wasn't very impressed with me.

Asuncion swung onto the bay gelding that she was riding. I climbed awkwardly into the saddle of

my horse, then followed her out into the pasture behind the shed.

"Wait!" a voice called.

Diego came out and stuck a grimy cowboy hat on my head. "There!" he said, with a wink. "That's more like it. You look like a real cowpoke now."

I felt a smile break out on my face. I pulled the brim down a little.

Mama would not have been happy if she had seen me in the hat. She believed that cowboy hats were for peasants and farmers.

Tata laughed. "Look at my little cowgirl!" he said. And for a moment I forgot about Estrella.

"Where to?" Asuncion said after we'd ridden out of the pasture.

"Don't you have a track or a trail or something?"

Asuncion made a face, like that was a really dumb idea. "Well. Yeah."

"I just meant...uh..." My voice sounded defensive. "Don't you have a regular place you ride?"

Asuncion waved vaguely toward the mountain that loomed over us.

"You just ride out there freely?" I said. I was a

little surprised. I was used to grown-ups planning everything I did. The notion of just riding randomly out into the hills made me a tiny bit nervous. "With no plan or trail or anything?"

Asuncion nodded.

And then I had an idea. "Have you ever heard of a place called Dimmind Rock?"

"Huh?" she said.

"Dimmind Rock," I repeated.

"You mean Diamond Rock."

I realized that the gang member who wrote the note must not have been a very good speller. "Yeah, that must be it. Diamond Rock. Why don't we go there?"

She looked at me strangely, then shrugged.

"Can we get there by ten?"

She shrugged again. "Maybe."

I felt a jolt of hope. If I could get there, I could do something to help get Estrella back. I couldn't imagine what that something would be. But I felt like I had to be there.

"Then let's go!" I said.

We rode off across the rocky landscape. It was hard riding, up and down steep hills, with no particular trail to follow as far as I could see. The valley that Cuernavaca is in is lush and green. But

Tata's ranch is a little to the west of the city. The further west you go, the drier the country gets. If you go far enough in the state of Morelos, you can see cactuses and other desert plants and animals.

Asuncion looked straight ahead and kept riding. She must have known about Estrella disappearing. But she never said anything about it, not even that she was sorry it happened. We must have ridden for twenty minutes when I noticed a figure in the distance. He was dressed completely in black. He sat motionless on a black horse at the crest of a hill off to our right. He was looking straight at us. For a moment I felt a little nervous.

I realized that for the first time in six months, Omar was nowhere near me. All those times back in Mexico City, I had wished I could ride by myself, without a bodyguard hanging around. But now we were totally alone in the middle of this rocky landscape. Anything could happen out here, and nobody would know. I looked around. I had no idea where I was. We might as well have been on the moon.

Suddenly the man snapped his reins and disappeared behind the hill.

"Who was that?" I said.

Asuncion looked at me. "Who was what?"

"There was a man riding over there," I said, pointing at the hill where he'd disappeared.

Asuncion shrugged.

I looked at my watch. It was 9:45.

"How much further?" I said.

Asuncion pointed. Maybe half a kilometer ahead of us, sticking straight up out of the ground, was a tall black rock that glistened in the sunlight.

"Wait," I said. "Is there any way to get close without being seen?"

She cocked her head and looked at me curiously. Finally, she pointed. I could see a small canyon running along the other side of Diamond Rock. I started to ride.

"Wait," she said. She took a pair of binoculars

out of her saddlebag, looked at the rock, then handed them to me. An old VW Bug was just pulling in next to the rock, throwing up cloud of dust.

Asuncion looked at me for a long time. "Are you gonna tell me what we're doing here?" she said finally.

"I think that man stole Estrella," I said. "He's part of a gang. They're ransoming her."

Her eyes lit up. "Really?"

I nodded.

I put the binoculars up to my eyes and watched the car stop. A man got out and looked around. He was wearing a black bandana across his face. A shiver of fear ran through my body.

"So what do you want to do?" Asuncion said.

"Uh…" I said. "I don't really know. I just want to make sure Estrella's okay."

"Does anybody else know about this?"

"Well, sure. The police know. Supposedly they're going to go negotiate with the gang to get the horse back."

"Let's ride around to that gully and watch!" she said.

I took one more look at the man in the black bandana. He was pacing up and down. I would have expected somebody who kidnapped horses for money to look composed. But he seemed a little nervous.

We rode around the hill, out of sight of Diamond Rock, then made our way along the bottom of a low, washed out gully. It was just deep enough that someone at Diamond Rock wouldn't have been able to see our heads.

When the rock finally loomed up over us, we dismounted and climbed up the side of the gully.

The man was still pacing around nervously. We were a lot closer now. I was worried he might see us.

"If he's got your horse," Asuncion said, "why didn't he bring her with him?"

"Maybe they're planning to exchange her for the money later," I said.

In the distance, I saw another car heading toward Diamond Rock. As it grew closer, I could see it was a police car.

The man in the black bandana hopped in his VW and started the car. It belched smoke, then began to drive away slowly.

"Oh, no!" I said. "This is terrible. If the police capture him, the rest of the gang will get mad!

They might hurt Estrella."

"They won't hurt her," Asuncion said. "She's worth too much money. The worst thing they'd do is try to sell her. You'd eventually find her."

"I hope so!" I said.

The VW continued to make its escape, picking up speed. There weren't really any roads here, just a big open space, with a few hills and gullies like the one we were in.

To avoid going into a gully, the VW reversed, turned around, and started tearing toward us. The ground was so rough that the VW bounced around like a toy. The wheels actually lifted into the air. I could see the man bouncing up and down in the seat. He was still heading in our direction.

"Uh-oh!" I said.

The police car was getting closer and closer, too. Dust was swirling everywhere now, making it hard to see.

"What do we do?" I said. I was starting to wish we'd brought Omar with us.

But before we had a chance to make a decision, the driver of the VW must have seen that he was about to run into the gully. He slammed on his brakes again, threw the car into reverse with a loud grinding of gears, and began backing up at full speed.

Then he disappeared into the swirling dust.

"Where is he going?" Asuncion said. "It looks like he's heading toward the—"

WHAM!

Before Asuncion could finish her sentence, the VW ran into something. When the dust cleared, we could see that the VW had smashed right into Diamond Rock.

The police car burst out of the swirling smoke.

The door of the VW opened and the man in the black bandana staggered out of the car. Then he began running.

Straight toward us!

I wanted to scramble back down the hill to the horses. But I froze. The man disappeared in the swirling dust again.

I could still hear his footsteps, though, getting closer and closer.

Asuncion grabbed my hand and squeezed. "Let's go!" she shouted.

But it was too late. The man appeared out of the dust. Silhouetted by the bright sun, he stopped right over us. His arms windmilled for a moment as he struggled to keep his balance and not fall

into the gully. The pointy toe of his worn old
cowboy boot was not more than half a meter from
my hand!

Two black eyes looked down at us from above
the black bandana. I don't know why, but suddenly
I didn't feel afraid. I just felt mad. This man had
stolen Estrella! I couldn't let him get away with it.

I reached out with one hand as he teetered
above me, grabbed his foot and yanked.

That was all it took. He lost his balance and
pitched over the edge, falling face forward onto the
ground below us.

For a moment he lay motionless.

"Ow," he said finally.

Then two policemen barreled over the edge of
the draw, jumped down the bank, and pinned him

to the ground.

"What?" the man said. "I didn't do anything!"

The bandana slipped off as the man was hauled to his feet. He was barely more than a boy himself.

I stared at him. "Hector?" I said.

CHAPTER FIVE

cinco

H is name is Hector," I said. "Hector Gutierrez. He works at my grandfather's ranch."

After the two uniformed police officers had pinned Hector to the ground, Sergeant Borges appeared out of the swirling dust. Unlike the night before, he was wearing a uniform, with high black boots, a shiny badge, a peaked cap with a shiny black brim, and very dark sunglasses. Sergeant Borges seemed to notice for the first time that Asuncion and I were clinging to the bank. "What are you girls doing here?" he said sharply, his whispery voice cutting through the air.

"We were just out riding," I said.

"Just out riding." I couldn't see the police sergeant's eyes, but I knew he was looking at me. His face showed no expression at all.

"Get back on your horses and go home," he said. "I need to question this man."

Hector was shaking with fear now. He seemed tiny next to the two strapping police officers. I had known Hector for as long as I'd been coming to the ranch. His father had been the stable manager before Asuncion's father took the job. Hector's father had died suddenly the year before. "I d-d-d-didn't do it!" Hector stuttered. "I was just...I was...I just w-w-wanted some money."

"Hector's all right. He does odd jobs around the ranch," Asuncion said. Sergeant Borges turned his dark glasses toward Asuncion. "I thought I told you girls to get on your horses and go home," he said.

We climbed down the bank and up onto the horses.

Tears rolled down Hector's face, and his teeth chattered. "Please!" he said, holding out his hands toward me. "P-p-please. Señorita Reña! Tell them! They have the wrong man. I would never hurt your h-h-horse!"

I looked at him for a minute. It was true. He was good-hearted. Sometimes he got in trouble at the ranch because he didn't have much sense, but there wasn't a mean bone in his body.

"Did you send the note, Hector?" Asuncion said. The way she said it, it sounded like she was talking to a little brother instead of a grown man.

Hector looked at the ground. He didn't answer.

"Hector!" Asuncion said.

Finally Hector nodded. "Señor Reña is gonna be so mad," he said softly. "And the Senator, too."

"So what happened to the horse?" Sergeant Borges said.

Hector shook his head. "I don't know. I never saw her. Everybody said she might have been kidnapped. So I thought I'd l-l-leave a note and they'd pay me. Senator Reña has a lot of m-m-money. He won't miss it."

Sergeant Borges stared at Hector for what seemed like a solid minute. The soft wind continued to blow across the dry ground.

Suddenly the sergeant seemed to make up his mind about something. He snapped his fingers at the other two policemen. "Put him in the car."

Then he turned to us.

"Go home."

Asuncion and I turned our horses and began riding back down the gully toward home. Now that the excitement was over, I felt a wave of disappointment run through me.

By the time we'd reached the end of the gully, the police were gone. Nothing was left but Hector's car, smashed against the huge black rock.

Asuncion sighed. "Poor Hector."

"Yeah," I said. "Poor Hector."

As we came up out of the gully, I saw a man on a horse riding out from behind the hill. He wasn't riding in our direction exactly. But he sure wasn't riding away from us either. He had a very loose, relaxed way of riding, almost like he was part of the horse.

"There!" I said. "Do you know who that is?"

Asuncion shook her head.

I tightened my knees, urging my horse to speed up a little. She shivered beneath me, then broke into a canter.

As the man grew closer, I saw that he was looking right at me. His eyes were piercing black. He was very handsome, in an unusual sort of way, and he had the dark skin and high cheekbones of an Indian. He wore a long leather holster attached to his belt.

As we drew even with him, he reached toward his holster. My heart started pounding. Oh no! I thought. He's got a gun!

But when he drew the object from his holster, I saw that it was not a gun at all. Instead it was a cane flute. And like his clothes, it was black, as though it had been charred in a fire. A ghost of a smile appeared on his lips, then he started playing

the flute. It was a strange tune, harsh and eerie sounding. He didn't look at us or acknowledge us in any way, even though we weren't more than twenty or thirty meters from him.

Then he was behind us. The haunting melody of the flute continued for several minutes, dying away eventually in the wind.

I looked around and the man was gone.

"Who was that?" I said nervously.

Asuncion shook her head.

CHAPTER SIX

seis

When we got home, Sergeant Borges's car was in the driveway.

Asuncion and I stabled the horses, then I went inside the house.

The servants were lined up like soldiers—the gardeners, the stable boy, the maids, the cook, my mother and father's bodyguards. Everybody.

Facing the lineup, Hector stood between the two brawny uniformed officers. His hands were cuffed behind his back and he was shivering. The servants shifted from one foot to the other and stared straight ahead. Sometimes they snuck nervous glances at Hector.

My grandfather was sitting in a straight-backed chair across the room, looking very serious. I went and sat down next to him. But he didn't look at or acknowledge me.

"It turns out," Sergeant Borges said to the servants, "that the ransom note was fake. This silly young man, Hector, thought he could get rich

off someone else's misfortunes. Instead he wasted
an entire morning of my valuable time. Now look
at him."

Everyone dutifully looked at Hector. His lower
lip was trembling and he didn't lift his gaze from
the floor. His face was bleeding from the fall into
the gully, and his clothes were dirty and torn.

"I'm done playing games!" Sergeant Borges
said. His strange voice cut through the air like a
whip. "People who play games with me will end up
in Hector's shoes."

Sergeant Borges walked up and down in front
of them, looking each one in the face. His shiny
black boots squeaked every time he took a step. He
was still wearing his sunglasses so you couldn't
see his eyes. His two large uniformed assistants
stood behind him with their arms crossed. I

wanted to find Estrella as much as anybody. But it seemed like Sergeant Borges was being unnecessarily mean to everybody.

"Tata—" I whispered.

But Tata raised one finger to signal that he didn't want me talking just then. I looked at his face. He was watching everything very intently. Usually Tata is really jolly around me. But at that moment he was stiff and formal.

"Does anybody here want to play games with me?" Sergeant Borges said. His whispery voice carried powerfully in the quiet room. "Huh? Anybody? Anybody?"

One of the gardeners smirked the tiniest bit and stifled a snicker.

Sergeant Borges looked at the man expressionlessly. "This seems funny to you?"

"No, sir!" the young man said, suddenly looking terrified.

"Take him outside," Sergeant Borges said.

The two uniformed officers grabbed the young gardener by his arms and roughly hustled him out the door. I looked at Tata to see if he'd react. But his face showed nothing at all.

"Anybody else have some clever commentary they'd like to offer?" Sergeant Borges said.

There was no answer.

"Good." He walked up and down the row of people, then finally stopped and pointed at Tata's maid. "You. Did you see the horse?"

"No, sir," she said, her voice trembling slightly. "I was making dinner."

Sergeant Borges walked slowly up and down the line asking each person in turn if they had seen Estrella. I wanted to shout, "Don't be so mean!" But I could tell that Tata would not be real happy if I did. So I just sat there with this knot in my stomach. For some reason I felt like it was my fault all these people were being put through this scary experience.

When he was done, Sergeant Borges stood there for a long time looking at everybody. "I don't think everybody here has been entirely truthful. I really don't. If I find that anybody is holding back information, that person is going to be very, very sorry."

No one spoke.

"Anybody with anything to add? Did anyone see the horse here at all—either inside the trailer or out?"

After a moment Hector raised his cuffed hands. "Sir? Your excellency? Sergeant?"

Sergeant Borges swiveled around and aimed his dark glasses at Hector's face.

"Sir? I saw the horse."

"You saw the horse," Sergeant Borges repeated.

"Yes, sir!" Hector's eyes were wide. "Yes, sir! I just r-r-remembered. I was cutting the grass. And I saw it in the horse trailer. I had to take the grass clippings around behind the barn. And when I got back, the door was open."

"You just remembered this."

"Yes!"

"And precisely why do you expect me to believe you after what you've just done?"

Hector looked away and shrugged meekly.

"You realize what you're saying, Hector?"

Hector looked puzzled.

"You're accusing one of these people of having stolen this lovely young lady's horse." The sergeant motioned in my direction. "This is not public property. There aren't people just wandering around here, coming and going as they please. A stranger would be noticed."

"I guess," Hector said.

Sergeant Borges gave Hector a cold smile. "So then you're accusing one of your friends."

Hector looked around desperately, like he was hoping someone would tell him what to say. "W-w-well...maybe I didn't see it."

Sergeant Borges looked at him for a long time without speaking.

After Sergeant Borges had dismissed the servants, he approached Tata. As he spoke, his entire attitude changed.

He took his sunglasses off. "Señor Reña," he said respectfully, "I have to tell you, I believe Hector when he says he saw the horse. I really don't think he's smart enough to tell a good lie."

"You're saying you think it was an inside job," Tata said.

"Yes, Señor."

"These people have been with me for years," Tata said. "I don't see how one of them could have done it."

"What about the Senator's bodyguards?"

Tata spread his hands. "They are my son's concern. I can't vouch for them."

The sergeant narrowed his eyes thoughtfully. "Are you suggesting you think it was one of the bodyguards?"

"I don't see one of my people doing it, that's

all," Tata said. "Where would they sell the horse? Who would they sell it to? It's a very high quality thoroughbred, an unusual horse. If they tried to sell it around here, I'd eventually find out."

"I agree, Señor," Sergeant Borges said. "I think I'll need to question the bodyguards more extensively. Do any of them know anything about horses?"

My grandfather looked at me.

"Only Omar," I said. "He rides with me."

The sergeant took out a notebook and wrote something in it.

"But he would never steal Estrella!" I said.

But all that the sergeant said was, "Thank you for your patience, Señor. We'll get to the bottom of this."

After the police were gone, I said to my grandfather, "Do you think Hector was telling the truth?"

Tata sighed. "Hector's a good kid. After he got caught, I think he was too scared to lie again."

"So do you think it's true what he said? That it's one of our bodyguards?"

Tata looked thoughtful. "I don't know who to believe."

"Could anybody have snuck onto the ranch and stolen her?" I said. I suddenly had a vision of the black-clad man on the horse that I'd seen while Asuncion and I were riding.

"Tell you what," Tata said. "Let's take a little ride together. I have something I'd like to check on."

After Tata left the room, my father walked in, talking on his cell phone. When he saw me he said, "I'll get back to you." Then he snapped his phone shut.

From the angry expression on his face I could tell he was mad at me. And I had a hunch I knew why. I hopped up and headed for the door.

"Where do you think you're going, young lady," he said. "Sit down!"

I sat, putting my hands between my knees and squeezing them tightly.

"What were you thinking, riding around without Omar to protect you?" he said angrily.

"This isn't Mexico City," I said. "Tata always says it's really safe around here."

"Tata has a very relaxed attitude about a lot of things," he said. "Besides, he's a grown man. You're only eleven years old."

"Yes, but—"

Papa cut me off. "Not only did you go out without Omar. You went out to where the horse was going to be ransomed."

"Yes, but it was just poor old Hector."

"That's not the point!" Papa said. "As far as you knew, you were meeting criminals!"

I looked at the floor. He was right. It probably had been a dumb thing to do. "I'm sorry," I said.

"Don't let this happen again," he said.

Mama came into the room. "And I don't like you playing with that girl, either. It doesn't look right for you to be mixing with the hired help."

"She's not the hired help," I said. "She's just helping her father for fun while she's out of school for the summer." Asuncion hadn't exactly been the most friendly girl in the world. But now I found myself defending her.

"It doesn't matter," Mama said. "It doesn't look right."

"Yes, Mama."

"And when you ride, I want you in proper riding clothes. You looked like a peasant in that ridiculous cowboy hat!"

"But I liked it!" I said.

"Don't talk back to your mother," Papa said. "Now go to your room."

CHAPTER SEVEN

siete

I sat in my room for a while. After a few moments there was a soft knock.

"What!" I said. I was in a bad mood.

The door opened and my grandfather peeped in. "Want to go riding now?" he said.

"Papa won't let me," I said.

Tata winked at me. "We'll sneak out!" he said in a loud, pretend whisper.

"Really?" I said.

"Your mother and father drove in to Cuernavaca," he said. "They won't mind if I'm with you."

I ran to the door and threw my arms around him. "You're the best!" I shouted.

Ten minutes later we were riding slowly out of the barn. "I hope you don't mind if I look like a peasant," my grandfather said, adjusting his cowboy hat with a grin.

"I don't know why Mama says things like

that," I said.

"Your mother is from an old family," he said. "Old families in Mexico look down on everybody who can't trace their lineage all the way back to Spain four hundred years ago. I don't take it personally. That's just how she was raised."

I nodded. "So where are we going?"

"I thought I'd show you something," he said.

But he didn't tell me what he was going to show me. Instead he started pointing out plants and animals and features of the land. It was very rough ground, and the horses had to work hard as we slowly climbed a trail that wound its way up a steep ridge. The air started getting cooler.

We must have ridden about eight kilometers when we finally got to the top of the ridge. A stiff wind blew over the top of the hill. In the distance, the Sierra de Ajusco mountain range loomed over us.

"Look!" Tata said, pointing at something on the other side of the ridge.

"What is it?"

"Wild horses," Tata said. "There's a herd of them up here."

We surveyed the area again. I looked back behind us. Tata's hacienda was barely visible in the distance. On the trail below us, I saw movement. It took me a moment to make out what it was. A black horse with a rider dressed in black. For a moment they were visible. Then they were gone.

"Have you ever seen a man riding around here on a black horse?" I said. "He wears all black clothes and carries a flute."

Tata frowned, then shook his head. "A flute?"

"A black flute made of cane. You know, like the Indians play."

Tata shook his head. "I don't think so, no. Why?"

"He's following us."

My grandfather didn't seem that interested. I noticed that even though the air was cool, he was sweating. And his face looked a little gray. I supposed that the ride was probably tiring him out.

"Are you okay?" I said.

"I'm fine," he said. "But we'd better get going if we're going to get there any time soon."

"We can go back if you want." I was still curious to know where he was taking me.

Tata just winked at me and started down the ridge toward the valley below us. "You will not want to miss this," he said.

My grandfather and I had been going for about half an hour when I heard the faint sound of guitars. "Is that where we're going?" I asked him.

Tata nodded as we came out from behind a stand of trees, then a huge smile spread across his face. There in front of us was a small village. The houses were cheap and ramshackle looking. Pigs and chickens rooted in the dirt around them. A dog lay sprawled in the sun.

But I understood why Tata was so happy. As poor as the town looked, I'd never seen such a scene. Everything about the place was bright and

cheerful. Clapping and dancing to the music, the women wore full skirts and short-sleeve shirts, embroidered with colorful designs. The men threw back their heads and laughed. They looked as if there was no place they'd rather be.

"Where are we?" I said.

"It's called Tlalnepantla," Tata said.

"Were you invited to the party?"

Tata nodded. "This is where I was born," he said. "I still have family here."

My eyes widened. "This is your family?" I asked.

"See that girl dancing in the middle of the crowd?" he asked. "She's my great-niece. Today is her fifteenth birthday."

"Her quinceañera?" I asked.

Tata nodded. "Let's go say hello."

Tata and I tied the horses up nearby and walked into the crowd. Quinceañeras are very important in Mexico. They celebrate a girl's fifteenth birthday, the time in her life she can take on more responsibility.

I had been to my sister Edith's quinceañera when I was just five years old. It had been nothing like the party in this village. My sister looked like a princess in her long white dress with a fluffy white skirt. White gloves covered her arms all the way past her elbows, and a sparkling tiara sat on top of her head. She and my mother had planned the whole event, which took place in a grand ballroom. Even though the most important people in Mexico were there, the biggest moment of the night was when Edith danced with my father. I could tell he was proud of her, and I had never seen my sister cry so much.

Ever since that day, I'd dreamed of having a quinceañera just like it. I had never realized there could be any other kind.

As we got closer to the celebration in Tlalnepantla, an old woman saw my grandfather and waved. She hobbled toward us, grinning with a toothless mouth. "Uncle Francisco!" she called.

"Uncle?" I said.

Tata introduced us. "This is my granddaughter, Pita. Pita, this is my niece and your cousin, Señora Reña."

"Hola, Señora," I said.

I couldn't help thinking that this was very strange. Tata's niece? She looked at least as old as he was.

Soon a crowd had gathered around us. Tata

seemed to know all their names. They treated him like he was a king. Some of them even kissed him on the hand.

Then Señora Reña pushed through the crowd, practically dragging the birthday girl behind her. "I made Rosa stop dancing so she could say hello to her uncle."

"Hola, Uncle Francisco," Rosa said. She wasn't wearing a puffy white dress or a tiara. She didn't even have on makeup or a fancy hairdo. Still, her smile nearly spread right off her face.

Tata took each of Rosa's hands in his. "How did you grow up so fast?" he asked her. "Last time I saw you, you could barely say my name. Now you are a woman!"

Rosa blushed, but she kept on smiling.

"Eat! Eat!" Señora Reña shouted.

I was more than happy to. The delicious smells of the tortillas, beans, and meat were making my stomach grumble. I realized that I hadn't eaten lunch.

I filled up my plate and sat down to eat. Between bites, I asked Tata the question that had been bouncing around in my brain. "You grew up here?"

"My father and mother were born here," Tata

began. "They moved to Cuernavaca right after I was born. Your great-grandfather got a job as a carpenter in the city. By the time I was grown, he had built a comfortable little business. He had several crews of carpenters. I apprenticed with him. Then I borrowed some money and built a house. I got lucky and made a little money on it. So I built another one. By the time I got married, I had made a pretty fair amount of money. By the time your father was born, I was a rich man. Your father was born, as they say, with a silver spoon in his mouth."

I couldn't believe it. How had I gotten to be eleven years old without knowing that my grandfather had come from a place like this? I had always known him as a rich and influential man.

My grandfather ate a few bites but didn't seem to have much appetite. But I ate and ate and ate and ate. And I didn't feel bad about it, either! My cousin sat down with us and chattered away with Tata, catching him up on news of the village. She told him about the crops and the rain and the animals they'd raised. A chicken had been born with two heads. A cow had died suddenly one night. The nopal (cactus) crop was good this year. She talked about spirits and omens.

Spirits and omens? I had the feeling that I had left the twenty-first century and traveled back in time.

My grandfather nodded as she talked but didn't say much himself.

When there was a lull in the conversation, I asked the old woman if she had ever seen a man who played a flute and rode a black horse.

She made the sign of the cross, moving her hands over her chest and face.

"You know him?" I said.

"He's not one of us," she said. Which didn't seem like much of an answer.

"Where does he live? What does he do?"

She shook her head. "Some people are afraid of him. They say he's a sorcerer."

"Do you think he's a sorcerer?" I said.

"He comes and goes," she said. "Sometimes he's gone for months. Then you see him in the distance. He never speaks. Once I heard his flute playing up in the woods. He plays the old tunes."

"The old tunes?" I said.

"She means the old Indian melodies," Tata said. "The songs no one sings much anymore."

The old woman nodded. "That's right. Our ancestors used to speak to the dead with the flute."

A shiver ran through me.

"The day after I heard his flute," she added, "old Señora Martinez had a fit and collapsed in her yard. She didn't walk again for almost two weeks."

Tata cleared his throat. "You know," he said, "I think we'd better go."

He stood unsteadily.

Señora Reña looked at him nervously. "Are you alright? You don't look good."

"I'm fine," he said, smiling.

"Why don't I get Alberto to drive you home in his truck."

Tata shook his head. "I've just got a little chest cold," he said. "I'll be fine."

But he wasn't fine. By the time we had reached the top of the ridge, heading back toward home, Tata was looking pale and sweat was pouring down his face.

"Can we stop for a minute?" he said.

"Sure, Tata," I said. I wasn't used to being consulted by adults. Usually they just told me what to do.

Tata looked back down the mountain toward Tlalnepantla.

"You know, your father has never been to the

village?" he said. His voice sounded weak.

"Why not?"

A funny look crossed his face. "I think he's embarrassed," he said. "He wouldn't want people to know that he's half-Indian, that his roots are so humble."

I supposed I could see why. Most people in Mexico have at least a little Indian blood in them. But, at least among people in our circle, nobody ever admits it.

Tata took off his hat and wiped his brow. "I think I should have taken up the offer of a ride," he said. He pressed on his chest with his hand. It looked like something was hurting him.

"Maybe we better go back," I said.

He shook his head. "We're almost home," he said.

We weren't really, though. We had at least another hour of riding in front of us. But I guess I could see his point. If he wasn't feeling good, it was still a long way back to the village. And then we'd be a fairly long car ride from the hacienda.

I was starting to feel really afraid. Tata seemed to be having trouble breathing now. It looked like he was fighting for each breath.

I tried to push my horse to go faster. But the

trail was very rough, and if the horses lost their footing, we could all fall down the side of the ridge. Besides, I could see Tata wincing with every step of his horse. He was obviously not in any shape to ride very fast.

What am I going to do? I kept thinking. I wasn't used to being responsible for anything. Usually there were people around me to do everything I needed. People washed my clothes. People drove me. People cooked my food.

Halfway down the mountain, Tata said, "I think I need to rest. Can you help me down?"

I scrambled off my horse and tried to help him down from the saddle. But I was too small to hold him and he fell as he tried to get his left boot out of the stirrup.

"Tata!" I shouted. He moaned, but didn't move.

His eyes opened. He blinked. There was something childlike about his expression, like a baby that didn't really know where it was.

"Pita?" he said finally.

"Tata!" I said. "What's wrong with you?"

He blinked again, sat up, wincing, then looked blankly around him. Finally he seemed to remember where he was. "Can you remember the way home?" he said.

"Why?" I said.

"I think you need to go get help." He took two long, gasping breaths. "Can you remember the way?"

I wasn't sure. Tata had been leading on the way out. And now that we were most of the way down the ridge, I couldn't see the hacienda anymore. There were trees and small hills in the way.

I was feeling panicky. What was I going to do? What if I got lost? What if—

A shadow fell across my face.

I looked up and saw a black-clad man on a black stallion. My heart jumped into my throat. He was looking down expressionlessly at me.

"Help," I said. "Can you help me?"

He didn't answer.

He just climbed off his horse and walked to my grandfather's side. He pushed gently on my grandfather's chest. Tata lay back on the ground. The man put his ear on Tata's chest.

After listening for a moment, the man in black sat up. Then he started trying to lift Tata to his feet. He crooked his finger at me, indicating that I should come over and help him lift Tata up. We supported Tata on each side and helped him toward the black horse.

"What's wrong with him?" I said desperately.

The man didn't answer. He just pointed at the black horse. It was a struggle, but finally we got Tata into the saddle of the black stallion.

The man swung smoothly up onto the horse, seating himself behind Tata, putting his arms around him so that he wouldn't fall. Then he snapped the reins and his horse leapt forward.

I was amazed at how fast he rode the horse. I did my best to keep up. But it was terrifying. I kept thinking the horse would stumble and I'd end up falling down the sheer face of the ridge. But we made it.

Then the man rode through the forest at the bottom of the hill. I could see the muscles in his back straining to hold Tata up. Tata's head was bobbling around. I couldn't tell if he was even conscious.

But the man didn't slow down. His horse was streaming sweat now from the strain of carrying the two men. But it didn't flag or stumble.

Please, please, please! I thought. *Please let us get to the hacienda in time.*

We came over a rise and then I could see Tata's house in the distance. "Hang on, Tata!" I called.

The horses' hooves thundered, and I hung on to my mount for dear life. We rode up a dirt track through Tata's peach orchard, then up behind the barn. The man in black reined in his horse, then lowered Tata to the ground. I leapt down to assist him. Tata was still conscious, but he was obviously very weak. He just lay there on the ground, looking up at me. His lips moved, but no sound came out.

"Somebody!" I called. "Somebody help."

"He's having a heart attack," the man in black said. "You'll need to call an ambulance now."

I realized it was the first time that he'd spoken. I had expected him to have a strong local accent. But he didn't. In fact, he sounded like an educated person from Mexico City. Before I could ask him anything else, the man jumped back onto his stallion and sped away.

"Help!" I called again.

Asuncion and her father burst out of the stable.

"What's going on?" Diego called to me.

"Tata's having a heart attack," I called back.

"Asuncion, call an ambulance," Diego said. He lifted Tata's head.

Tata's lips were still moving. A hoarse sound came from his throat.

"What's he saying?" Asuncion's father said.

"I don't know," I said.

After Asuncion disappeared, my mother and father came out of the house. They both looked annoyed.

"What's all this noise?" Mama said.

"Where have you been?" Papa called angrily to me.

"With Tata," I said.

"And what in the world are you wearing, Pita?" Mama said, seeing the cowboy hat and jeans I was wearing. "How many times have I told you—"

It was only then that she and my father spotted Tata lying on the lush grass.

"Oh, no!" Mama said.

"What's wrong with him?" Papa said, eyes widening.

"I think he's having a heart attack," I said.

Mama and Papa both crouched over him. Tata grabbed hold of my father's hand and pulled him closer. His lips were still moving.

"What?" Papa said. "I can't hear you."

Tata's lips continued to move. His eyes were looking up at my father like there was something important he wanted to tell him. My mother leaned over him and put her ear next to his mouth.

She frowned and looked at my father.

"What?" Papa said.

"It sounds like he said—" She kept frowning and didn't finish her sentence.

"What?" Papa repeated.

"It sounded like he said, 'Octavio.'"

"Octavio?" Suddenly my father's face went stiff.

Then he stood up and yelled. "Somebody call an ambulance! Why isn't anybody calling for an ambulance?"

CHAPTER EIGHT

ocho

A helicopter flew out from Cuernavaca and picked up my grandfather, then Papa and Mama drove off in the car to meet him at the hospital.

Before she left, though, my mother said, "Where were you?"

"Tata and I went for a ride."

Mama glared at me. "Didn't your father tell you not to go riding alone?"

"But I was with Tata! He said it was okay."

She pointed her finger at me. "You know better. You should be ashamed of yourself. I'm very angry!"

I lay in my bed crying the rest of the afternoon. First my horse and now this. My grandfather was just about my favorite person in the world. He had always seemed so strong and healthy to me. It had never even occurred to me that he could get sick. What if he died?

It was all my fault!

The main reason I had wanted to go riding with Tata was because I was hoping that I might be able to find Estrella. If it hadn't been for that, I probably would have just told him that today wasn't a good day, or that Mama and Papa wouldn't let me go. And then Tata wouldn't have tired himself out. And then maybe he wouldn't have had the heart attack. Or at least he could have gotten to the hospital a lot quicker.

When Evita came and told me that it was dinnertime, I told her I didn't feel like eating. After a while she finally brought me some food. But I couldn't eat it. I just left it on the dresser.

After a while someone knocked on the door.

"Who is it?" I called out weakly. When no one answered, I got up and went to the door. I opened it, but no one was there. Lying on the floor, though, was a pile of my favorite magazines.

I looked furtively up and down the hallway. Who could have left them for me? And how could they have known how much I loved them?

One thing was certain—it wasn't my mother. She hates magazines full of stories about movie stars and celebrities as much as I love them.

I grabbed the magazines, closed the door, and lay down to read. When I read the magazines, I find myself in a place that seems more glamorous and elegant than the world I live in. Which is kind of odd, I guess. Some people would look at my life and think it was glamorous. But the truth is, it's like being in a cage. It's a nice cage, but...

Well, it's my life. What can I do?

The next morning Mama and Papa were at the breakfast table when I came out. They looked at me gravely.

"How's he doing?" I asked.

Papa nodded. "He's doing okay. He's stable. We have the best doctors in Cuernavaca working on him." Papa's voice broke slightly and he looked away from me. I had never seen my father show that kind of emotion before.

We sat in silence as Tata's maid served my breakfast. Papa recovered himself, but he just stared straight ahead and finished eating. When he was done, he rested his hands on the edge of the table.

I put my spoon down. "May I ask a question?" I said.

"Sure," my father said.

"Who is Octavio?"

There was a brief silence.

"Nobody."

"But yesterday you said that—"

"Your Tata was sick," my mother said sharply. "He was probably hallucinating."

I could tell from her expression that she wasn't telling me the truth, though. There were two little red spots on her cheeks, like she was angry about something. I knew enough not to ask anything else. My mother is no fun when she's angry!

"Why don't you go out and play," she said. "Omar can take you riding."

"I don't want to go riding with Omar!" I said. I don't know why it came out like that. Omar's very nice. I just didn't feel like it.

There was another brief silence.

Then my father said to my mother, "There's no reason not to tell her."

My mother pursed her lips. She never disagrees with my father—not around other people anyway.

My father turned to me and said, "Octavio is my brother."

"Your brother!" I said. "You don't have a brother." My father came from a large family. He had seven sisters, I knew. But no brother.

"My brother," he said again.

I looked at my father, then at my mother, then at my father. My father looked at my mother, like he was looking for help.

"Don't look at me," she said, putting down her napkin, standing up and walking away.

My father sighed loudly. "Your grandfather was married to another woman before he was married to your grandmother," he said.

I shrugged. "Okay."

"Look," he said. "In this country people make a big deal about your family background. Where you came from. What your social status is. Right?"

"I guess," I said.

"Well, your grandfather's first wife came from a very poor background. She lived in a little village way out in the country. They had a son named Octavio. Then she died. Between the time that they married and the time that she died, your grandfather became a very successful man. When he remarried my mother—well, my mother was from an old family in Cuernavaca. Very old fashioned. And she didn't like having Octavio around. He was sort of a reminder of your grandfather's ... humble background. It made her uncomfortable. So she sent Octavio off to boarding school in the United States. We hardly ever saw him."

"That seems kind of mean!" I said.

"It was. But those were different times back then." Papa looked out the window. "Anyway, things were tough between Octavio and my father. When Octavio came home, they'd get in fights. Eventually Octavio and my father just stopped communicating. I haven't seen him in thirty years. I honestly don't even know if he's still alive."

"That's so sad," I said.

Papa nodded sadly. "You know, the saddest thing is that I always felt like Octavio was more like my father than I was. He was an athlete. He was funny. All my life I always felt like, underneath all that fighting, Octavio was really my father's favorite son. Then, yesterday, when he looked up at me and thought I was Octavio..." Papa took a sip of his coffee. "Well, it brought back a lot of sad memories."

This was very strange. Not just what he was telling me...but the fact that he was telling it to me at all. My father never talked to me about grown-up things. Whenever there were grown-up things to discuss, he would say, "Pita, run along. We have things to discuss." And off I would go.

Papa's sad look faded. He went back to his usual stern face. "So where did you and your grandfather go yesterday? Your mother was worried sick."

I cleared my throat. "He took me to Tlalnepantla."

Papa stared at me accusingly.

"How was I supposed to know?" I said. "I'm just a kid! He said, 'Let's go for a ride.' So I went."

"Well, Tata's full of surprises this week, isn't he? For a moment Papa was silent, then finally he said, "Well, you're a brave girl. You got him home all by yourself. You probably saved his life." He smiled at me. "I'm very proud of you, Pita."

Proud? I can't remember the last time Papa had said something like that. I beamed back at him. "Actually I didn't do it all myself. There was this—"

Papa's cell phone rang. "Hello?" he answered, stepping out of the room.

"As soon as your father is finished with his call, we're leaving for the hospital," Mama said.

"Can I come?"

Mama shook her head. "Not today. Hospitals are not suitable places for children."

She walked to the door, then paused, her hand on the knob.

"Be good. And no riding. I'm very serious."

"But—"

"No buts!" she said. "If you go anywhere outside this house, I want Omar with you." She turned and walked swiftly out of the room.

After breakfast I walked out of the kitchen. Omar was standing in the living room talking in hushed tones on his cell phone. I thought I heard him say the name Estrella. But I wasn't sure.

"I have to go," he said hurriedly, flipping his phone closed.

I had heard Mama chewing him out for not being with me when I went riding with Tata the day before. Omar looked at me nervously. "Where are you going, Pita?" he said.

"Out to the stable."

"No riding!" he said. "Your mother has made it completely clear."

"I'm just going out to look at the horses."

"Then I'm coming with you."

"I'm just going out to—"

"I have strict instructions," he said coldly.

I went out to the stables and found Asuncion and her father feeding the horses.

"Can I help?" I said.

Asuncion gave me a bag of oats, then followed me as I went over and fed the horse I'd ridden with my grandfather.

"I'm sorry about your grandfather," she said after a minute.

"Thanks," I said.

She looked at me, then said, "Did you get the magazines I left for you?"

I blinked. "That was you?" I said.

She nodded.

"How did you know I love them?"

She wrinkled her nose and giggled. "Me too!"

I gave her a quick hug. She looked sort of

flustered.

I said, "I can't believe that..."

The next thing you knew, we were talking like we'd been friends forever. It turned out we had a lot in common. We were both great at math but hated history. And of course, we both loved reading—especially magazines—and horses.

As we were talking, Omar kept making phone calls. Whenever he talked, he cupped his hands over the phone and turned away from us, like he didn't want us to hear what he was saying.

After a while, I said, "You seem really different today."

"What do you mean?" Asuncion said.

"Well, yesterday you seemed kind of...uh...not very friendly."

Asuncion's face colored a little. "I guess I thought you'd be stuck up," she said.

"Why?" I said.

She shrugged. "You're a Senator's daughter. My dad works for your grandfather. I guess I thought—" She didn't finish her sentence.

I sighed. "Yeah, I know," I said.

On the other side of the stable, Omar was drumming his fingers and watching us.

Asuncion leaned toward me and said, "What's

the deal with him?"

"He's my bodyguard."

"I know that," Asuncion said, laughing. "I mean, he keeps looking all guilty when he talks on his phone."

"I don't know," I said. "I was noticing that, too."

Asuncion lowered her voice to a whisper. "What if he's the one?"

I was puzzled. "What one?"

"You know! The one who stole your horse."

I shook my head and laughed. "That's silly. Omar's a really nice guy."

"Well of course he's nice to you," she said.

"What do you mean?"

Asuncion made a face. "Come on, you know what I'm talking about. It's his job to act nice to you. If he was mean to you, you might say something bad to your father. And then he'd get fired."

"He's not like that!" I said.

"How do you know?"

I thought about it. The truth was, I didn't know.

"Let's investigate!" Asuncion said. "Maybe he'll lead us to Estrella."

"Investigate?" I said. "How?"

She smiled. "Just watch!"

CHAPTER NINE

nueve

I'll need a distraction," Asuncion had said.

"What kind of distraction?" I said.

"Something that will get your grandfather's security guards outside."

"What for?"

"Just wait." She grinned. "Big distraction. Okay? Big!" Then she walked away.

A big distraction, I thought. Okay.

My heart started thumping hard as I walked outside. Omar put his hand over his cell phone. "Where are you going?" he called.

I pointed out toward the peach orchard. There was nothing to see in the orchard. Nothing but squirrels, jumping from tree to tree.

Omar looked over at the orchard, then went back to his phone call. The peach orchard was the key to my plan. But I wasn't going there. Not yet anyway.

I doubled back around the barn, then ran over

to the house and in the back door. Maximilian stood at the door, yapping like crazy.

"Look, Max," I said, pointing toward the peach orchard. "Squirrels!"

Maximilian is barely bigger than a squirrel. But boy does he love chasing them. I don't know what he thinks he'll do if he ever catches one!

I looked around to make sure that no one was watching, then I opened the door and nudged him with my foot. He didn't take any prodding, though. He could smell those squirrels. The next thing I knew, he was off like a little furry orange rocket, racing across the lawn toward the peach trees.

I watched him for about thirty seconds, then yelled, "Help! Help!"

Maids and cooks and security guards started appearing from all over the place.

"What's wrong? What's wrong?" everyone was shouting.

"Help, everybody! Maximilian got out!"

Everyone suddenly looked a little irritated. They obviously thought I was being hysterical.

"Mama will go crazy!" I cried.

Two of the security guards looked at each other and sighed. They knew I was right.

I burst out the door and started running

toward the peach orchard. "Help!" I shouted.
"Everybody help me get Maximilian back."

The two guards tore past me, determined
looks on their faces. Nobody wanted my mother
mad. I looked behind me. Everybody in the house
was streaming after me—cooks, maids, security
guards. Everybody.

And ahead of us, streaking across the grass
toward his paradise of squirrels, was an orange
ball of fur.

"Come here, Max!" a security guard coaxed.

"Here boy!" Omar yelled.

Which, as I knew, was a total waste of time. Omar probably did, too. Max didn't listen to anybody. Not even my mother. He wouldn't sit. He wouldn't stay. He wouldn't roll over or fetch or come when you called. Max did whatever Max wanted.

I have to tell you, it was pretty funny! There must have been ten or twelve people running out into the peach orchard. The thing I knew that they didn't was that once Max got bored with the squirrels, he'd come trotting back and start scratching on the back door to get inside again.

Big brawny bodyguards were tripping over each other and diving at the dog, who scampered off, looking indignantly over his shoulder at them.

"Got it!" a voice behind me said.

I turned around and there was Asuncion.

"Got what?" I said. "What's the big secret?"

Asuncion held up a small electronic device that looked like a walkie-talkie. Only it had a lot more buttons and lights. "What's that?" I said.

"It's called a frequency scanner," she said. "You can use it to listen to people's cell phone conversations. I figure if Omar's talking about Estrella on the phone, we can listen in and find out what he knows."

"But where did you get it?"

"Your grandfather's security guards used it. There was an employee on the ranch who was stealing farm equipment and selling it to somebody. But they never could catch him at it. So they got this and recorded his conversations with the person he was selling it to." She waggled the little scanner in the air. "This put him in jail."

"How does it work?"

She shrugged. "I'm not really sure."

"Well, let's just turn it on and see what happens."

Asuncion thumbed the switch and a row of lights came on.

Over in the peach orchard, one of the bodyguards lifted Max triumphantly in the air. Max was yapping and yapping. Suddenly he started peeing. The bodyguard dropped the dog and jumped away.

Everybody started laughing and pointing at him. Then the chase was on again.

"I feel a little bad," I said, watching everybody running around the orchard.

Asuncion and I looked at each other. Then we burst out laughing. And in that moment, I knew I had a new best friend.

Eventually they brought Max back. Asuncion and I volunteered to comb all the leaves and twigs out of his coat—since it was actually our fault he got out in the first place.

"We'll take him back to my room," I said.

Asuncion and I went to my room and closed the door, then set up the little scanner. A row of lights kept flickering. But nothing came out except static.

"I wonder if it's working," I said.

"Maybe there's just nobody around talking on a phone," she said.

I sat down with the comb and began the tedious task of combing all the junk out of Max's coat. Asuncion started flipping through the magazines, reading all about stars from telenovelas—in America they call them "soap operas"—and showing me dresses that everybody was wearing at award ceremonies.

The two of us laughed and joked, and after a while we pretty much forgot about the scanner, which continued to emit a steady, dull hiss.

Suddenly, there was a crackling noise, and the hissing stopped. We both sat up straight.

"Elena?" an urgent voice said. "It's me, Omar."

I grabbed Asuncion's arm. My heart was in my throat.

"Omar!" the voice said. "Whatcha doin'?"

"You wouldn't believe it," Omar said. "I spent all morning chasing a stupid dog around. Pita set the stupid thing loose on purpose and then sat around laughing while everybody in the house chased it. Then it peed on my best suit."

I looked at Asuncion. "Oops!" I said, flushing.

"How did he know?" Asuncion said.

I shook my head.

"So," Omar said. "You free for dinner after I get off work?"

"Sure."

Asuncion scowled. "Gross! It's just his girlfriend."

Omar and his girlfriend chattered on for a few minutes, then he hung up.

"Now I feel terrible," I said. "Everybody must think I was just making fun of them."

"Hey, don't worry about it. Everybody likes you here."

"Plus, I feel a little weird about eavesdropping on him talking to his girlfriend. It seems kind of creepy."

Asuncion gave me a serious look. "Do you want to find Estrella?"

"Well, sure."

"We're not doing this for kicks. We're trying to find out what happened to your horse."

"Yeah," I said. "I guess…"

The scanner crackled again.

This time it was the cook talking to her mother. It made me feel very uncomfortable. They didn't discuss anything really personal or anything embarrassing. But still….

As I picked through Max's coat, the scanner crackled, with one phone call after another. Girlfriends, children, mothers—but nothing that would help me find Estrella.

Finally Max was all fixed up and Asuncion had gone through all the magazines. We were getting a little bored.

"We can't just sit here all day," I said.

"Yeah, but—"

The scanner crackled again.

"Hello?" a voice said. An odd, whispery voice.

"Sergeant? It's me, Omar. Have you found out anything else?"

"We're still working on it."

"The Senator will pay a lot of money for that horse," Omar said.

"What's your point?"

"You're not cutting me out of this."

"Did I say anything about cutting you out?" the Sergeant said.

"I've done my part. Why haven't you?"

"Ransom is a risky possibility. Things can go wrong. Selling the horse is the safest avenue. That's why I'm—"

"I need this," Omar said. "I've got a money situation that—"

"Everybody has a money situation," Sergeant Borges said. "When I have something to tell you, I'll tell you."

There was a brief pause, then Sergeant Borges said, "Wait. I'm getting some information now. I'll call you back in five minutes."

The scanner lights flickered, and the line went dead. I stared at Asuncion.

"Sergeant Borges must have Estrella!" I said. "What are we going to do?"

"We have to tell your father."

"But when he finds out that we took the scanner and everything, he's going to..." My words faded in my throat.

We sat motionless for several minutes, our heads not more than a few inches from the scanner.

When the scanner finally *bleeped,* we both

jumped.

"Omar." It was Sergeant Borges. "I think maybe we can resolve this. There's a little Indian village out in the boonies. It's near Tlalnepantla. Meet me there."

"Why there?"

"There's a guy there—Look, I'm not going to explain it all on the phone. Just be there."

"I'm working," Omar said. "I'm guarding the Senator's girl."

"This whole thing's getting too hot. We need to make it go away. Now are you in or out?"

"Alright. Alright. I'll be there."

The scanner light blinked off.

"Oh, my gosh!" I said. "What do you think they're going to do?"

"It sounds like they're going to get rid of Estrella," Asuncion said. "What are we going to do?"

Get rid of Estrella? Did that mean they were going to—

Before we could answer the question, there was a knock on the door. I quickly hid the scanner under a blanket.

"Yes?" I called.

Omar opened the door. "Pita, an emergency's

come up," he said. "I have to go take care of something. I want you to stay here until I'm back."

"Sure," I said.

"Your grandfather's security guards are here to take care of you. But I don't want you setting foot outside until I'm back. Okay?"

I nodded.

Omar narrowed his eyes and pointed his finger at me. "I've told everybody in the house to keep an eye on you. Not one foot out that door. Are we clear?"

I swallowed. "Uh. Okay."

We sat there in silence as his footsteps faded down the hallways.

"We have to get to Tlalnepantla!" I whispered.

"But how?" Asuncion said.

I opened the door. One of Tata's security guards, Hugo, was sitting at the end of the hallway. He smiled at me. "Where are you going?" Hugo said.

"Who me?" I said, a knot forming in my gut. "Nowhere."

CHAPTER TEN

diez

So we didn't have much choice, did we? We climbed out the window, across the slippery red tiles of the roof, over the garage and down a trellis on the far side of the house.

My heart was slamming in my chest. If we'd slipped off the roof, we'd have broken some bones for sure. But we made it safely.

Tata's gardener was out in the yard trimming roses and humming to himself. He stood right between the stables and us.

"Do you think Omar told him you're not supposed to be out here?" Asuncion whispered.

"I don't know," I told her. "We'd better not take the chance."

"I'll go talk to him," she said. "While we're talking, you sneak across the yard behind us to the stables."

I watched as she walked over to the gardener and started making conversation. I looked around, then tiptoed across the grass. It seemed as if every blade of grass made a tiny sound as I slowly moved from foot to foot.

Asuncion laughed loudly and pointed at something. The gardener laughed, too. I kept going.

Suddenly a voice behind me called, "Hey! Pita! Where are you going?"

It was Hugo!

I froze. Asuncion whipped around, looking at me, then at Hugo.

"Omar left me with strict instructions," Hugo called. "Come on! Inside!"

All I could think about was Estrella. What if they were getting ready to sell Estrella? Or worse!

Without thinking, I started running toward the stables.

"Hey," Hugo yelled. "Get back here, Pita!"

I thundered into the barn and looked around. The smell of oats and hay and horses surrounded me. The horses were stirring around nervously as I pounded across the floor. I looked behind me. Asuncion was right there.

"What are we gonna do?" she called. "There's no time to saddle the horses."

"We'll have to go bareback!" I shouted.

I opened the stall of the horse I'd been riding

the day before, then climbed up on the stall and
jumped onto the horse. She stirred and whinnied
nervously. She wasn't used to having anybody on
her back without a saddle and bridle.

I put my head against her neck, wrapped my
arms around her and kicked her flanks with my
heels. She didn't move.

Hugo came into the stable. "Pita, your mother
and father are going to be very angry!" he yelled,
panting.

"Do you know how to ride bareback?"
Asuncion called to me.

"I have no idea!" I said. My heart was racing
and my hands trembled.

"Me either!" she called.

I kicked the mare again. Hard. This time
she reared up. "Go!" I shouted. "Run! Gallop! Do
something!"

And she did. The horse rocketed out of the stall, wheeled around and then tore out of the stable. She seemed as confused and nervous as I felt.

And riding bareback on a galloping horse was the scariest thing I'd ever done in my life.

"Pita! Pita, you get back here!" voices were yelling after me. I looked back and saw Hugo running after me. Behind him, half of Tata's staff was streaming out of the house, all of them yelling my name. They looked really mad!

And then Asuncion's horse came charging out of the stable, its pale mane and tail waving in the breeze. Asuncion had her head down and her arms wrapped around its neck. She was grinning from ear to ear.

"Whooooooo!" Asuncion yelled as we thundered down the trail. "We're in deeeeeep trouble now!"

She came up beside me, and all I could think about was staying on the horse. Riding a galloping horse was scary enough. Without a saddle, it was totally out of control!

But I felt completely free, too. The muscles of the big horse moved easily under me and I felt faster than the wind. There was no time to think about Mama or Papa or Omar or Hugo—or even Estrella. Every fiber in my body was concentrating on staying on that horse.

And what's really cool is that I did. I almost fell twice. But each time I managed to hang on and tell the mare where I wanted her to go. The only way it could have been more magical would have been if it had been Estrella.

After a minute or two, the horses slowed to a trot. Then after another minute they slowed to a walk. They were breathing hard.

I patted my horse on the shoulder. "Good girl," I whispered into the horse's ear. "Good girl! You did great!"

We rode for a while without speaking.

Finally I looked over at my new best friend. Our eyes met. We understood each other perfectly.

For a minute, I felt like I wasn't a little girl anymore. I felt grown-up and strong, like I didn't have to ask anybody for permission every time I wanted to go somewhere or do something. I knew it wasn't true. I knew that when I got back— whether we rescued Estrella or not—I was going to be in bigger trouble than I'd ever been in my life.

But for a second it felt like something big had changed. I felt like a different person.

"*That* was scary!" Asuncion said.

"Yeah," I said.

We didn't speak for about thirty seconds.

Then we started laughing and laughing and laughing. I thought we'd never stop.

Tata must have ridden to Tlalnepantla a bunch, because the horses seemed to know the way. Pretty soon we had crested the big ridge and descended into the valley where the little village was located.

"That's where my grandfather was born," I said.

"You're kidding!" Asuncion said. "I never would have thought that a rich old guy like him—" She broke off, looking slightly embarrassed.

"—would have come from a little Indian village?" I said.

"I guess, yeah."

"Just goes to show you, huh?" I said.

As we descended the mountain, I saw a dust cloud coming up off the dirt road that led to the village.

"There's Sergeant Borges's car," I said. "We better hurry."

"Um...what are we going to do when we get

there?" Asuncion said.

"If they have Estrella here, then I'll try to get her away from them," I said. "That's about all I can do."

"Do you have a cell phone?" Asuncion asked. "You could call your dad."

"Yeah," I said, pulling my phone out of my pocket and looking at it. "Darn it! There's no signal in this valley."

Asuncion and I continued down until we reached the village. We found some rope and tied our horses to some bushes then snuck forward around a pigpen. Sergeant Borges's car was just pulling in. We ducked behind the pigpen just as he screeched to a halt.

The doors opened and Sergeant Borges climbed out, scanning the village from behind his dark glasses.

As we were hiding, one of the pigs came up and began snuffling loudly next to us. Sergeant Borges looked in our direction. I couldn't tell if he was looking at the pig or at us crouched down low on the other side of the fence. I squeezed my body in tighter, wishing I could make myself invisible.

"Pigs!" he said, nearly spitting. Then he turned his head as a man came out of the door of a nearby house. He took off his hat as he approached Sergeant Borges.

"Your Excellency," the man said, "you made good time."

The police sergeant said, "Spare me the flattery. Where's the horse?"

"Sir?"

"The horse. You told me on the phone you had the horse."

"Oh!" The man nodded. "Yes. Right, no. I don't have the horse."

Sergeant Borges looked at his men. "Did this man drag me all the way out here to waste my time?"

"No, no, no," the man said urgently. "I know where it is. A brown horse with a white face, right? Very tall? Very beautiful?"

"That's the one."

Estrella was alive! And she was right here.

"I know where it is," the man said.

"Show me."

The man took two steps, pointed off toward Tres Marias Mountain, which loomed over us in the distance. "There," he said.

Sergeant Borges stared into the distance. Finally he said, "I don't see a horse."

"There's a herd of wild horses up there," the man said. "The horse you're looking for is with them."

"Somewhere up in that one hundred square kilometers of rugged mountainside, there's a horse." His voice dripped sarcasm.

The man's smile faded, and he cleared his throat. "Will I get the reward?"

"The reward was for returning the horse to Senator Reña. You don't have the horse." Sergeant Borges looked straight ahead and thought a moment.

Who would know how to find this herd of horses?" he asked.

The man's shoulders went up and down. "I don't know, sir." He looked thoughtful. "Well, there is one man."

As he was talking, Omar's pick-up truck pulled in behind Sergeant Borges's car.

"What have you found out?" he called hopefully. "Have you got her?"

Sergeant Borges shook his head disgustedly. "This man says she's joined a herd of wild horses in the hills."

Omar looked as downcast as the man from the village. "I need to find this horse. I'm a trained bodyguard. I spent ten years in the Army. I've got all kinds of training and expertise in martial arts. And I can't even keep an eleven-year-old girl from getting away from me."

"What's that got to do with the horse?" Sergeant Borges asked.

"Getting that horse back will prove to the Senator that I can handle a big job—that I can guard him."

I blinked. So I had this whole thing wrong. Sergeant Borges and Omar weren't doing anything shady at all! They were just trying to do their jobs and get Estrella back. I felt terrible for having suspected the worst of them.

"What are we going to do?" Omar asked Sergeant Borges.

"We need a guide," Sergeant Borges said. "Somebody who could help us find this herd of wild horses."

Omar looked at the man who had called Sergeant Borges out to the village. "Can you take us up there?"

The man shook his head. "Not me, sir. That's rough country up there. It was just a coincidence that those horses got close to the village. They could be anywhere by now. You need somebody with a horse. If you go on foot, it'll take you forever."

Sergeant Borges sighed and shrugged. "We'll find the horse eventually," he said. There was a brief silence. Omar and the Sergeant shook hands glumly and began to say good-bye.

Then I heard an odd whistling noise in the distance. It was so far away that I could barely make it out. Then I realized what it was. It was the sound of a cane flute.

Suddenly an idea hit me. I stood up from behind the pen.

Omar stared at me. For a moment his face was blank with surprise. Then he looked furious. "Pita!" he said. "What are you doing here? "

"Wait," I said. "Before you get mad, I have an idea."

once

There's a man who lives up there," I said, pointing. "I bet he could help us."

"I'm taking you home," Omar said grimly.

"Wait, wait, wait!" I said desperately. "Think about it. If we go home without Estrella, we're both in trouble. If we find her, we're heroes."

Omar ran his hands through his hair. "Who's this man?" he said finally.

"I don't know his name," I said. "He plays an Indian flute and rides a black horse. Listen."

Everyone turned their ears up to the mountainside where I was pointing. The distant sound of the flute was almost lost in the soft wind.

The man from the village shook his head. "Oh, the flute man. He's a sorcerer. I don't think you want him to help you."

"He saved Tata's life yesterday," I said. "I think he'll help us—if we can find him."

Asuncion and I borrowed a pair of ancient saddles from the villagers, and Omar mounted a sway-backed old mare. We rode up the trail toward the flute sounds.

It didn't take long before we found the man in black. He was sitting on a stump playing his cane flute and looking off into the distance.

When he heard us, he stopped playing. He looked at me with an odd, searching expression. "Well, hello again," he said quietly. "How is the old man?"

"I think he's doing okay," I said. "He's in the hospital now."

The man looked at the ground without speaking.

"Why did you ride off without talking to anybody?" I said.

The man didn't answer.

Omar looked impatient. "Look, Señor," he said. "There's a herd of horses up there. Do you think you could help us find them?"

The man nodded. "Well, what a coincidence," he said.

"What's that mean?" Omar said sharply. I could tell he was in a bad mood. He wanted to find the horses and get back to the house pronto.

"Nothing," the man said.

"What's your name?" Omar said.

The man gave Omar a long, cool look. "My name is Octavio Reña," he said.

My eyes widened. "You're my uncle!" I said.

"Your uncle!" Omar said. "What are you talking about?"

The black-clad man looked off into the distance. "Yes," he said. "I guess I am. You must be Agapita?"

"Pita," I said. "They call me Pita." I looked at him closely. "Why do you live out here?"

"I'm a wildlife biologist," he said. "I teach at a university in the United States. I'm doing research here."

"Research?"

"I study wild horses. This herd appeared only a few years ago. It's very strange. So I decided to study them. I come down a few times a year, camp out up in the mountains and follow them."

"Oh," I said. "Why don't you ever visit my grandfather?"

Octavio looked into the distance before

answering. "There wouldn't be any point. We don't get along."

"That's dumb," I said. "All the horses in the world that you could study, and you choose a herd five kilometers from your own father's house? That sounds like more than just an accident."

Octavio looked a little irritated. "You think?"

"It sounds to me like you wanted to see your family. But you were scared or felt weird or something. So you just sat up here in the mountains and kept hoping you'd run into them or something."

Octavio's face clouded for a moment. Then he laughed and looked at Omar. "She's a little psychologist, huh?"

Omar looked at his watch.

"You saved his life yesterday, you know," I said.

My uncle didn't say anything. His smile faded.

"Why don't you come over and have dinner with us?" I said.

He shook his head. "No. We'd just end up fighting."

"When was the last time you talked to Tata?" I said.

"Thirty years, I guess."

I laughed loudly.

"What?" he said.

"Don't you think things might have changed a little after all that time?"

He didn't answer.

"Come on!" I said. "Please! Pretty please!" I clasped my hands together and pushed out my lower lip like I was really sad. "Come and have dinner with us."

My uncle started laughing. "Alright, alright, alright. I'll come for dinner. But that's all." He put his flute away and mounted his horse. "If you want to find them by sundown, we'd better get moving."

After we'd ridden for a few minutes, he stopped and pointed. "There," he said. "You see them?"

I saw a whirl of bodies on a distant ridge. It was impossible to make out any individual horses, though. I wondered what it would be like to be one of them. How would it feel with no one to tell you when you could come and go, or where you were supposed to be.

"Here, take my field glasses," my uncle said, handing me a pair of binoculars.

I aimed them at the far ridge and found the

herd. They were mostly brown and black horses. But one horse was easily spotted because of her white face. I felt a burst of happiness. "Estrella!" I shouted. "She's there!"

"Yay!" Asuncion yelled.

"Let's go get her!" My voice echoed off the hillside.

"It's not quite as easy as all that," said my uncle. "This is treacherous country. We can't get across this area." He pointed at the rocky slope below us. "We'll have to circle around and come up behind them."

Omar scowled and looked at his watch. "We need to get the show on the road."

"There's no quick way to do this," Octavio said. "If you want the horse—"

Omar nodded glumly.

We rode along the ridge, then eventually down into the valley. As we descended, we lost sight of the herd of wild horses behind the trees.

The hillsides were starting to get very rocky, and the horses started getting nervous. All the loose rocks made their footing uncertain, and my horse slipped several times. One time I would have fallen off the horse if Omar hadn't reached out and grabbed me and boosted me back onto the horse, my heart slamming in my ribs.

The shadows started getting longer, and the air began to chill. We were higher in the mountains now, and the temperatures were dropping. I realized that I wasn't really dressed for this.

I looked over at Asuncion. She smiled at me. But I could see she was a little scared, too.

The light was beginning to slant sharply through the trees by the time we got to the top of the second ridge. This one was more like a small mountain, rising much higher than the ridge on the other side of the valley.

"Your mother and father are not going to be happy with me," Omar said, looking at his watch for about the billionth time.

And then my uncle held up his hand. We all stopped. He cocked his head.

"You hear it?" he whispered.

I didn't hear anything but the wind in the

trees. But then, there it was—a distant whinny!

"They're there!" I said.

Uncle Octavio turned to Omar and Asuncion. "You two need to wait here. If we all try to approach, you'll spook the herd and they'll run off."

Omar shook his head. "If anything bad happens— "

"Nothing bad is going to happen," Octavio said softly. "The herd knows me. But Estrella doesn't. Pita needs to come. Estrella will come to her."

Omar's face looked about as sour as a lemon. But he knew my uncle was right.

"Don't ride straight at them," my uncle said

as we began riding forward. "Once we start getting close, you'll want to dismount and just walk slowly out. Did you bring any food? A carrot? Oats? Anything?"

I shook my head.

"Well, then you'll just have to call to her and trust that she comes to you."

The horses were grazing on a grassy slope about a hundred meters in front of us. One of the horses spotted us then. It snuffled and all the horses looked around and stared at us, their ears going back and their nostrils sniffing at the wind.

"Stop," Uncle Octavio said softly. "We don't want to scare them. They're very skittish. They don't trust people."

I stopped and watched the herd.

"Breathe slowly, Pita," Uncle Octavio advised. "Be calm and they won't feel threatened."

My pulse thrummed in my veins. I breathed in, then out. It seemed like time was stretching like taffy.

"I'm going to turn around and leave you," my uncle said. "Wait a minute. Then dismount and walk very slowly toward them. Don't make any sudden moves or lift your arms. If they get restless, just stop moving. Be patient. When you think Estrella is close enough to you to recognize you, just call to her."

I nodded. My uncle turned his horse slowly. I could hear his horse's hooves scrabbling on the rocky mountainside as he rode slowly away. But I didn't look back. All my attention was focused on the herd. I could see Estrella among them. She didn't seem different from them, though. She looked just as nervous as they did.

I counted my breaths. After fifty breaths, I climbed off my horse. The herd stirred and moved around nervously.

I just stood there for a while. I was getting pretty cold. But I didn't really think about it. My whole brain was focused on the herd. Not just Estrella, but the whole herd. Which is kind of strange, you know? I felt like I understood something about them, though I couldn't tell you what it was. It was like there was an invisible string connecting me to them.

And eventually the string began to pull me toward them. I started walking slowly across the top of the ridge. One step. Then another. Then another.

When I'd gone about fifty meters, I stopped. For maybe the first time in my whole life, I felt totally alone. The rough wilderness stretched out around me. For a minute I believed that if I just kept walking, I could be part of the herd and never go home. I could just wander around in the mountains forever.

I envied those beautiful animals, coming and going however and whenever they wanted, with nothing to worry about but eating and sleeping. I took some more deep breaths. I felt calm now. Calm, but sharp.

I walked forward a few more strides and stopped.

In the distance, the big red sun was settling into the jagged mountains in the west.

Now I could see Estrella clearly. She sniffed the air. Horses don't see all that fabulously, but their sense of smell is good. The wind was moving in her direction and I could tell that she smelled me. Her tail twitched and she cocked her head like she was surprised to see me.

For a second I thought about just leaving her there, enjoying freedom with the other wild horses. But she wasn't meant to live out there. She'd eventually starve or get hurt.

It was time.

"Estrella," I called softly. "Estrella. Time to go home, girl."

Estrella shook her mane and looked around at the other horses. She'd tasted freedom now. Would she even come to me at all? For a moment, I wasn't sure.

Estrella nuzzled one of the other horses, like she was saying good-bye.

Then she came toward me.

doce

I t was well after dark when the four of us finally got home with Estrella.

I had expected everyone to be frantic. But it turned out that Omar had called ahead and told them that everything was okay. With Tata being sick and our getting Estrella back, I guess Mama and Papa didn't feel like chewing us out too much.

Plus, there was Octavio. That kind of took the heat off of me.

I walked in the door and said, "I brought someone with me."

Octavio stood there in the doorway, holding his dusty hat in his hands.

My mother frowned. She must have been wondering who this dusty guy was. I guess she had never even met him. But my father just stared at him for a long time.

"How's Dad?" Octavio said.

"We're bringing him home in the morning," Papa said. "He's doing well."

My uncle shook his head gravely.

"Well, come in, then," Papa said. "Can you stay for dinner?"

"Just for dinner," my uncle said. "Just for dinner."

Aren't families strange?

Later I asked Uncle Octavio why he didn't get along with the rest of the family.

"I'm like a wild horse," he said. "I don't take well to the bridle."

"What's that mean?" I said.

"This is a very correct family," he said. "There's a right way and a wrong way. Everybody in this family always does the correct thing. Except me. I could never do the correct thing. Your father was always the good student, the star athlete, the guy who did everything right. I was the one who always got in trouble. I was the one who did things my own way."

For the rest of the summer, Asuncion and I rode up into the hills with Uncle Octavio and watched the wild horses. After a while we started helping him take notes and measurements. He never made us feel like little kids.

We saw a foal being born. We saw an old

female die. We saw them eating and sleeping and playing.

After a while I started to understand what Uncle Octavio was trying to find out in his studies. He wanted to know if wild horses could survive here. It just wasn't the normal place for them.

Finally, as the summer was coming to a close, I asked him, "Do you think they'll make it?"

Uncle Octavio, I had learned, was not the world's most talkative guy. He looked thoughtfully at the horses and shrugged.

"Maybe there's no future for wild horses," I said. "Cuernavaca keeps getting bigger and bigger. Pretty soon there will be houses and stuff out here. People retiring from the United States. Rich people from Mexico City building vacation homes."

Still, Octavio didn't answer.

Uncle Octavio, Asuncion, and I were sitting about a hundred meters away from the horses, watching them graze. Suddenly the horses looked up, eyes wide, ears pinned back. They whirled and, with a thunder of hooves, tore over the crest of the hill and disappeared.

"What do you think they just heard?" I said. "What was it that scared them?"

But Uncle Octavio just shrugged again.

We never found out exactly what had happened to Estrella. Somebody must have opened the trailer door and then gotten distracted. While nobody was looking, Estrella must have just galloped off into the hills. And when she found the wild horses, she just became part of the herd.

We're heading back to Mexico City tomorrow. Back to all my friends. Back to my normal life. Back to my school uniform. Back to bodyguards and chauffeured cars and a house with a huge wall around it. Back to my English riding boots and my jodhpurs and my English saddle. Back to riding in the same big circle on the same trail every day at the riding club.

But it won't be quite the same.

Because I've ridden with the wild horses.

Meet The Rest of the Karito Kids™

Now that you've read Pita's exciting adventure, *Mexico Mystery*, check out the other Karito Kids™ Adventures. Let us introduce you to:

Wan Ling from Shanghai, China in *Shanghai Secret*:

Moving to a new city can end up being one big adventure for any 11-year-old girl around the world. But I think I got more than my share of excitement. I don't know why – maybe it's me and my curiosity, maybe it's the unusual job my father has, maybe it's my love for the pandas. What I do know is that I was just trying to fit in after being forced to move to Shanghai with my parents and grandmother – and that's when the mystery began to unfold!

> **Zai Jian** *(this means goodbye in Chinese)*,
> Ling

Lulu Rehema Kibwana from Nairobi, Kenya in *Nairobi Nightmare*:

Everyone tells me how lucky I am to be on a kid's TV show in Nairobi, Kenya. They're right: It is a brilliant job, especially because I get to talk a lot about my favorite sport, football (that's soccer in North America). But when a famous statue was stolen while the show was on the air and my friend was accused of doing it, I had to do something. So, join me on my quest through Nairobi to find the real thief.

> **Kwaheri** *(this means goodbye in Swahili)*,
> Lulu

Zoe Nicole Linden from New York City, USA
in *The Manhattan Menace*

My mom tells me that we have to leave New York, the city I absolutely love. I can't leave my best friend Hana, my favorite used clothing store, riding the subway...it's totally crazylicious (that's one of the made-up words I'm famous for)! My mom will lose the brownstone that she's been trying to fix up and we won't have enough money to stay if Hana and I can't find the missing tiara that had been hidden somewhere in the brownstone. The clock is ticking and I'm running out of time!

Later,
Zoe

Gia Valentina Russo from Florence, Italy
in *Florence Fiasco*

You wouldn't believe all the excitement at our little pensione in Florence, Italy. A dream came true for me as a future fashion diva: One of the greatest designers of all time was staying at our inn. Well, it was a dream... until it became a nightmare. The beautiful shoes created by the famous Franco del Sarto couldn't be found and he was blaming me for stealing them! It took me and my American friend, who loves fashion as much as I do, to fearlessly fix this fashion fiasco.

Ciao *(this means goodbye in Italian),*
Gia

You can also enjoy each of these characters as 21-inch play dolls with beautiful faces and very cool fashions! Go to www.karitokids.com to find out more.

Even though Cuernavaca is where my heart is, I spend a
lot of time in Mexico City which is a very different place.
I think you'll understand if you read some of the stuff
I've written in my journal.

16

Mexicans are so beautiful. We are actually
a blend of Spanish and over 60 different
South American native peoples.

People were in Mexico long long before me. In lots
of places you see modern skyscrapers right next
to churches built 400 years ago. Even more amazing:
there are pyramids left by our Aztec and Mayan
ancestors that are over 2,000 years old. And they
keep finding ruins under the square in
MEXICO CITY!!!

Mexicans are party people! Especially my family because Papa (my father) works so much he needs a break. My family celebrates El Dia de la Bandera (Fiesta of the Mexican Flag) on February 24th. I think it's cool how the colors in the Mexican flag each stand for something: green stands for independence, white is for religion, and red is for national unity. But, *mi abuelo* (grandfather) reminded me to be most proud of the meaning of those colors: hope, purity and union.

Mi abuelo also shared the story about the shield that is on the flag. According to legend our ancestors, the Aztecs, were told by the gods to establish a city where they find an eagle perched on a prickly pear tree (cactus) eating a snake. I bet that doesn't happen every day! But they saw it on the swampland of what is now Zocalo, the square in Mexico City.

September 16th in Mexico is kind of like the 4th of July in the U.S. We shoot off fireworks and play music and dance in the streets to celebrate our independence from Spain. Every year El Presidente steps out on the palace balcony and rings the famous liberty bell that was used to rally the people to fight for independence. Then he shouts "Viva Mexico!" and "Viva la independencia!" And everybody shouts it back and throws tons of confetti and red, white, and green streamers all over the place. It's totally crazy and lots of fun.

Cuernavaca is my favorite place in the world. It is about being free: free from schoolwork and all the noise and craziness of the big city. Whenever we come here, I remember how very lucky I am in this life. People love to vacation in Cuernavaca, which is called "the city of eternal spring" because the weather is so great all year round. They love to stroll around the beautiful parks and gardens full of tropical plants and flowers. But for me it's about being at *el ranchito*, taking care of the horses and riding out into the hills...riding like the wind!

Estrella

Today we went to Chapultepec Park. It's a lot like Central Park in NYC. There are lakes, a huge zoo, an amusement park and museum, and pushcarts selling ice cream, *aguas frescas* (fresh fruit drinks) and my favorite: shaved ice with sweet syrup called *raspados*!!!

My favorite holiday is the Day of the Dead, El Dia Des Los Muertos. But it is so misunderstood! It's not sad or spooky. It's a celebration of life. We remember people we loved who have passed on...even our favorite pets. And we talk about what we loved about them or how funny they were. Our family has a big dinner party. Bread of the dead *(pan de muerto)* is always on the table and a plastic toy skeleton is hidden in every loaf! It's considered good luck if you bite into one.

My class is studying the Aztec civilization, so we went to the ancient city of Teotihuacán. It's about 25 miles from my school, so we take a hired bus for the trip. You get to climb a huge pyramid there called Pyramid of the Sun (the third largest pyramid in the world) and walk down the Calle de los Muertos (street of the dead).

The best things to eat:
My favorite meal is called mole poblano.
It's chicken with a fantastic sauce, mole,
which is flavored with Mexican chocolate.

And heaven on earth is crepas de cajeta:
paper-thin pancakes (crepes) covered in goat's
milk caramel sauce. Oh yes, and I'm crazy
about camotes: a soft, chewy candy made from
sweet potatoes.

I also love tacos, especially tacos al pastor from
the taqueria near our house. These tacos are
not ground beef. They're made with pork that is
marinated and slow-roasted on a spit.

I love Diego Rivera. He's one of Mexico's most famous artists. On the side of the Palacio Nacionale, home of the Mexican government, you can see gigantic murals that he created. It took 16 years (with a little help from his assistants!) to paint the walls of the palace with fantastic scenes showing Rivera's view of the history of Mexican culture and civilization.

Hola (O-La) = Hello
Por Favor (Pour-fah-vohr) = Please
Gracias (Grah-see-ahs) = Thank you
Que Tal (kay-tul) = How are you?
Hasta Luego (Ahh-stah Loo-way-go) = See you later
Adios (Ah-dee-Os) = Goodbye